Meghan Rose
and the
Not-So-Silent Night

written by
Lori Z. Scott

illustrated by
Stacy Curtis

Standard®
PUBLISHING

Cincinnati, Ohio

Published by Standard Publishing, Cincinnati, Ohio
www.standardpub.com

Text Copyright © 2012 by Lori Z. Scott
Illustrations Copyright © 2012 by Stacy Curtis

Printed in: USA
Project editor: Diane Stortz

ISBN 978-0-7847-3578-7

Library of Congress Cataloging-in-Publication Data

Scott, Lori Z., 1965-
  Meghan Rose and the not-so-silent night / written by Lori Z.
Scott ; illustrated by Stacy Curtis.
      p. cm.
  Summary: When icy roads strand Meghan, her parents, and
friend Kayla in a noisy church fellowship hall on Christmas
Eve, Meghan comes to understand the true meaning of
Christmas.
  ISBN 978-0-7847-3578-7 (pbk.)
[1. Christian life--Fiction. 2. Christmas--Fiction. 3.
Automobile travel--Fiction.] I. Title.
  PZ7.S42675Mag 2012
  [Fic]--dc23
                                    2012021302

18 17 16 15 14 13 12   9 8 7 6 5 4 3 2 1

Contents

Blue-boo-hoo Christmas without You

"Open it up." My friend Ryan gave me what my dad calls a goofy grin.

I shook the present Ryan gave me. "What is it? A Pickle-brand pen?"

Ryan shook his head. His grin grew bigger—what Dad calls ear to ear.

"Is it a Purr-purr Pretty Kitty poster?"

"No," Ryan said. His grin grew bigger—what Dad calls a mile wide.

"Something with . . . Super Cat?"

Ryan's grin grew even bigger. I don't think Dad has a name for a grin like that. I call it where did your lips go?

"Open it already!" Ryan said.

"OK!" I ripped off the wrapping paper fast as a Christmas shopper grabs a deal. "An empty paper towel roll?" I said in a sidewalk-flat voice. "Wow."

"I put your gift *inside* the roll to protect it," Ryan said. "I was thinking about you and your long trip down to Texas to visit your grandparents for Christmas."

"We're stopping in Missouri to see my Aunt Joy too," I said.

Ryan took the paper towel tube and pulled out curly papers stapled together like a book. "I thought you might get bored in the car, so I wrote a Super Cat adventure comic for you. My brother helped with the writing, but I drew the pictures all by myself."

"Wowie!" I said. "Thanks!"

"I'll probably draw more comics since you won't be here to play with me," Ryan said.

"And I'll have a blue-boo-hoo Christmas without you," I said.

The doorbell rang. "That's probably Kayla," my mom called from the kitchen.

"Whoo-hoo!" I yelled.

The day before, Kayla's family had a family emergency. My mom said Kayla's parents needed to rush to the hospital in a town near ours for "we're-not-sure-exactly-how-long," and they couldn't take Kayla with them. So Kayla would be driving to Texas with us instead!

Ryan raced me zippy-quick to the door and yanked it open. Cold air smacked my face. Kayla and her parents stood on the doorstep. Kayla had a stuffed duck in one hand and a suitcase in the other.

"Kayla!" I yelled, pushing past Ryan.

Mom came up behind me and took the suitcase. "Good to see you, Kayla. There are some Christmas cookies in the kitchen I need to get rid of. Why don't you kids help eat them?"

Kayla and Ryan took off. I stayed behind to put Ryan's gift safely on the entryway table. That's when I heard Mom say, "How much have you told Kayla?"

I froze in place like a snowman. When Mom told me Kayla would spend Christmas with us, I was so excited that I never bothered to ask about the emergency. What was it?

"She knows that her grandma is very sick and that we have to go to the hospital immediately," said Kayla's mom. "But she doesn't understand why she can't come with us."

My heart went BUMP-bump. A sick grandma! Oh no! I bet Kayla would feel extra blue-boo-hoo too.

"We're praying for you," Mom said.

"Thank you. You don't know how much I appreciate this," Kayla's mom said in a shaky voice. "I feel horrible being apart from Kayla at Christmas. Are you sure this is OK?"

"No problem at all," Mom said. "We love Kayla like she was our own daughter. And she'll get to celebrate Christmas with you when things settle down."

Kayla's mom tried to smile. "At least Kayla's excited about being with Meghan. That will go a long way to making her feel better."

Just then, Kayla and Ryan burst out of the kitchen. Kayla had red frosting smeared on her lips. Her cheeks puffed out like a chipmunk. "Ffanks for fa foofies!" she yelled. Cookie crumbs shot out of her mouth like tiny firecrackers.

Mom laughed. "You're welcome."

"You're lucky, Meghan," Ryan said. "My brother has a basketball tournament over Christmas break, so we're stuck here."

"At least Illinois will probably get snow," I said. "I don't think it snows in Texas."

That idea made me frown. Wasn't snow the most important thing about Christmas besides presents? Snow and presents *and* decorating. I had a special Meghan-made garland packed away to help decorate Grandma's house.

Kayla interrupted my frowning with a loud "QUACK!"

We laughed and laughed. Good friends are like that. Just when you are feeling boo-hoo blue, they quack you up.

Mom's phone buzzed. "Ryan, it's your mom. Time to go home."

Kayla's mom said, "Come give us a hug, Kayla. It's time for us to leave too."

I followed Ryan into the yard while Kayla said goodbye to her parents. The almost-cold-enough-for-snow air made my skin go bumpy.

"Enjoy my present!" Ryan called, running to his house next door.

"See you in two weeks," I called back.

Even though what I wanted to see in ONE DAY was *snow*.

It's Beginning to Look a Lot like Christmas

We left early the next morning. While we drove, Kayla and I watched a movie. Then we played "I Spy," a game with license plates, and the Quiet Game—which lasted about three seconds.

Finally I said, "I'm bored."

"Watch a movie," Mom said.

"I only brought one," I said. "And believe me, no one wants to watch *Froo Froo, the Happy-Yappy Poodle's Yip-Yappy Christmas* more than once."

"Let's listen to Christmas music on the radio," Mom said.

So we listened to Christmas songs and sang them at the top of our lungs. And that means LOUD.

Plus, we spotted fun decorations. Flashing lights. Silver bells. Wreaths. Tin soldiers. Fat Santas. Candy canes. Trees. Angels. Trumpets. Snowmen. Reindeer. Gingerbread men. Everywhere we looked was beginning to look a lot like Christmas. And that reminded me about my special surprise. "I can't wait to decorate Grandma's house with my Meghan-made garland."

"What's a garland?" Kayla asked.

"It's like a necklace made for a giant," I said. "You string together leaves or pinecones or popcorn or paper loops. Then you hang it someplace."

"What did you use?" Kayla asked.

I gave Kayla a sneaky grin. "It's a secret. You'll have to wait until we get to Grandma Thompson's house before you see it."

Suddenly Kayla squealed, "Oh! Is THAT a garland, over that church door?"

I looked out the window. "Yes! Right!"

The church yard had a Christmas display, with Mary and Joseph sitting by a crib. Plus, they had a real donkey and lambs—and a cat.

"Kayla, let's read Ryan's Super Cat comic!" I squealed.

The adventure went like this:

Our hero, Super Cat, must find the *purr*fect Christmas gift for his friend Clawdia. But as soon as he arrives at the mall, Super Cat knows something is wrong.

The Christmas music is stuck on "The Twelve Days of Christmas," playing it over and over. Which makes it about 12,000 days of Christmas instead. Which is ridiculous. And annoying.

Christmas lights have been rearranged to spell "Merry Chicken."

The "Visit Santa" signs lead to the restrooms.

In place of nuts, clusters of grapes sit by the nutcrackers. Now the nutcrackers go SQUISH instead of CRACK and make sticky messes.

Sale signs have been changed. One by the socks now says, "Buy one pair, get 77 pairs FREE!" Signs by popular toys say, "GO AWAY."

"This is the work of the fowl Poultry Gang," says Super Cat.

"How do you know?" Clawdia says.

Super Cat jumps and screams. He didn't expect to see Clawdia at the mall, let alone appear behind him.

Striking a superpose, Super Cat thrusts a business card into Clawdia's paws. It says, "*This mall mess is brought to you today by the Poultry Gang and by the letter Z.*"

"And that's not all," says Super Cat, pointing. "Look!"

Several sneaky-looking chickens are hiding behind a snowman display. They are armed with feathers. And they're reading a book called *How to Launch a Tickle Attack in the Mall* by

Dr. H. A. Ha.

The gang tosses aside the book and starts their attack at a Tarbucks store.

"Oh no!" Clawdia cries. "Not the coffee shop!"

Giggling breaks out. Then loud hee-hee-ho-ho-hos. Coffee spills. Shirts get stained.

It's coffee chaos.

"They must be stopped," Super Cat says. "But how? My usual weapons—armpit odor, hairball pellets, and fish-smell spray—are useless here because . . . well, the mall is already filled with armpit odor, hairball pellets, and fish smell. And that didn't stop the Poultry Gang!"

Super Cat searches for an idea.

Ah-ha! He grabs a harp from a decorative angel. Then he snatches a box of peppermint sticks from a nearby candy store.

"That will be $21.56," says a voice. It's the candy store clerk.

"But this is a police emergency!" yells Super Cat.

"Will that be cash or credit?" the clerk asks.

Super Cat digs around in his pockets. He throws a wad of cash on the counter.

"One . . ." says the clerk, smoothing out a dollar bill. "Two . . . By the way, do you have any pennies? I'm short on change. Three—"

"ARGH!" yells Super Cat.

"I'll deal with this," says Clawdia.

"You stop the Poultry Gang."

Clawdia takes out her credit card and charges.

Quickly, Super Cat licks a peppermint stick, loads it into the harp, aims, and *Fffooommm!* The wet candy shoots SMACK into its feathery target. And sticks.

"Huh?" says the struck chicken. Then *FOOM, FOOM, FOOM!* He's hit with more sticky peppermint candies. The extra sugar weight topples him to the floor with a squawk.

"It's working," Clawdia cheers as she tucks away her receipt. "Let me help. I'll lick them, you stick them!"

The battle soon ends. With the Poultry Gang out of business, business at the mall returns to normal. Except for one thing. The grapes stay in place of the nuts. The store thinks the switch will get people with nut allergies to buy nutcrackers.

Once again, Super Cat saves the day. Plus, now he has minty-fresh breath.

The end.

Kayla and I gave a happy sigh. "Now THAT'S a great Christmas story," Kayla said.

3

Do You BAM! Hear What I Hear?

"I loved Ryan's adventure," I said.

"Me too," Kayla said. "But I've got one question. Are we there yet?"

"We have about an hour to go until Aunt Joy's house," Dad said. "The good news is, there's plenty of Christmas music on the radio."

"No thanks," I said. "If I hear 'Rudolph the Red-Nosed Reindeer' one more time, I'll have nightmares about noses."

Kayla held up her stuffed animal. "Mr.

Thompson, Duck wants you tell us a Christmas story instead."

"Sure," Dad said, clicking the radio off. "Do you have a favorite?"

"How the Grinch Stole Christmas," Kayla said. "By Dr. Seuss."

"Really?" Dad said in a low, growly voice. He stuck out his lip in a pout and scowled at us in the rearview mirror. "Do I look like a grinch?"

We both laughed at his creepy voice and funny-looking face.

But I didn't want that story. Ever since I saw the Mary and Joseph display in front of the tiny church, I'd been thinking about it. It wasn't flashy or LOUD or sparkly, but it made me feel warm and quiet and happy. Like the way you feel when you're snuggled up cozy in your bed at night.

"Tell the *real* Christmas story," I said. "The one with Mary and Joseph in it."

Kayla looked confused. "You mean Mary and Joseph were *real?* I always thought Jesus' birthday was just a story."

"Jesus' birthday really happened," Dad said. "It happened long ago in a part of the world far from where we live. The Grinch, Rudolph, Frosty . . . those fictional stories are a fun part of America's Christmas tradition. But Jesus' birthday is the whole reason we celebrate Christmas. Do you want to hear about it?"

Kayla nodded.

"OK," Dad said. "Keep in mind that even though it happened about two thousand years ago, the story is still important today. It's as fresh as milk and cookies."

"I wouldn't drink two-thousand-year-old

milk," Kayla said. "Yuck!"

"You would if the milk never spoiled and the cookies stayed warm," Dad said. "When you listen to the story, remember that it doesn't have an expiration date. The story starts with a visit from an angel named Gabriel."

"An angel! Did he play for Los Angeles?" Kayla asked. "Did he give out autographs?"

Dad laughed. "No. He was an *actual angel.* God sent him to visit a girl named Mary who lived in Israel, that far-off place I told you about. He told Mary, 'Hello! Don't be afraid of me! God wants me to tell you something special.'"

"That's better than an autograph," I said, nudging Kayla.

"Then Gabriel told Mary she was going to have a baby boy," Dad said, "and that she

22

should name him Jesus."

"I would have named him Billy Bob," I said.

"I would have named him Duck," Kayla said.

I made a huffy sound. "You name everything Duck," I said.

Kayla shrugged.

"Well," Dad continued, "Gabriel told Mary to name the baby Jesus. And he said that Jesus would be God's own Son. And that he would have a kingdom that would never end."

"Like milk that never expires?" Kayla asked.

Dad nodded. "Yes. What do you think Mary said when she heard this news?"

"I'll need some diapers?" Kayla said.

"No," Dad said. "Mary said, 'May it

happen just as God said.' And that was a very brave thing to say, because she was engaged but not yet married. Gabriel also told Mary that her cousin Elizabeth would have a baby boy. That was amazing news because Elizabeth was very old—too old to have a baby."

"Did Elizabeth have a cat?" Kayla asked.

"Uh . . ." Dad said.

"Because my great-aunt is too old to have kids," Kayla said. "So she has a cat instead. She dresses it up sometimes and feeds it fancy food. She calls it her widdle baby."

Just then, something went *BAM!* Mom screamed, my heart went BUMP-bump, and the car swerved. Dad gripped the wheel and pulled off the road. With a WUMP-WUMP-WUMP, our car slowed down.

"Everyone OK?" Dad said.

I gave Kayla a quick look. Her eyes were big and wild and she was squeezing Duck tight. So things looked normal. "Yes," I said. "What happened?"

"We've got a flat tire," Dad said. "The rest of our story will have to wait."

Car-Jack Frost Nipping at Your Nose

"Hello, Joy?" Mom said, talking loudly into her cell phone. "Yes, it's me! We've got a flat tire. We'll drive on the spare to the next exit and find a service station. No, go ahead with dinner. We'll find a place to eat while we're waiting. Love you too."

Sighing, I peeked out the window. For once, I was glad it wasn't snowing. Otherwise Dad would be BRRRR-cold changing the tire.

I guess if he got too cold, he could use my garland for a jump rope. All that hopping around would heat him up.

Dad put on our car blinkers. I love how car blinkers blink and click at the same time. It makes me feel like a giant four-door lightning bug.

"This car is packed as tight as six elephants squeezed into an elevator!" Dad said. "I can't reach the spare tire unless I take things out and put them by the side of the road."

Kayla held her stuffed duck even closer. I patted her shoulder. "Don't worry," I said. "He won't take Duck."

"What's that?" Kayla said, pointing. Dad had something in his hands.

"That lifts the car so we can take off the flat tire," Mom said. "It's called a car jack."

Kayla leaned over and whispered in my ear, "I would have called it a car duck."

"Jack is better," I whispered back. "Can you imagine people passing us and saying, 'Look at that car. It's being held up by a car duck'? That just sounds weird."

When the spare was on, Dad reloaded the car and we drove to the next exit.

"There's a service garage," Mom said.

"Plus, there's a Burger Palace restaurant right next to it," I said. "Yay! Beefy burgers on a bun with mustard-pickles-ketchup and fun, fun, fun!"

"I want a kid's hamburger meal!" Kayla yelled.

"Me too!"

"Me three!" Mom said. "I love the prizes."

We all laughed at that.

We left the car at the service station and walked over to Burger Palace.

"How long will it take to fix the tire?" Mom asked as we sat down.

"I don't know," Dad said, handing out our food. "They'll text me when it's ready."

Duck sat in the chair next to Kayla. Kayla gave him three long French fries.

"Do you want to pray?" Dad asked me.

I nodded. "Dear God, please help our tire to get fixed zippy-quick. Please keep Kayla's parents safe. Please take care of grandmas everywhere in the world."

"Bless ducks everywhere too," Kayla added.

"Ducks too," I said.

"And friends," Kayla said.

"Friends too," I said.

"And car jacks," Kayla said.

"And travelers," Dad said.

"What about the food?" Mom whispered.

"And bless car jacks and travelers and our food." I opened one eye. "Did I forget anything else?"

Three heads shook no, and we all said, "Amen."

"Can you tell us more of the Christmas story while we eat?" Kayla asked. "Duck would like that."

Dad grinned. "Well, we can't disappoint Duck, can we? Let's see . . . when we left off, Mary had just talked to an angel and found out she was going to have a baby boy who was God's own Son. After that, Mary went to her cousin Elizabeth's house for three months."

"That's a long visit," I said. "Just think how much I would miss my friends if we stayed in Texas for three months."

"What about Joseph?" Kayla asked. She talked with her mouth full of hamburger. "Did Joseph visit Elizabeth too?"

"No," Dad said. "In fact, when Joseph learned that Mary was expecting a baby before their marriage had taken place, he wondered if he should call off the wedding. But then an angel appeared to Joseph in a dream—"

"Was it Gabriel again?" Kayla asked.

Dad shrugged. "I don't know. The Bible doesn't tell us."

"Then I'm calling that angel Duck," Kayla said.

"OK . . ." Dad said slowly. "Then the angel—"

"Named DUCK," Kayla interrupted.

"—told Joseph that he should still marry

Mary," Dad said. "And he explained that God picked Mary to be the mother of his Son. What do you suppose Joseph did when he woke up?"

"He bought diapers?" Kayla said.

"No," Dad said. "He did what the angel told him to do. He married Mary!"

Just then, Dad's cell phone buzzed. He checked it, then said, "I'll stop our story there for now. Let's finish up and use the restrooms. Our car is ready to go."

5

Here Comes Meghan Rose

"Here comes Meghan Rose, here comes Meghan Rose, right down Meghan Rose Lane!" I sang as we turned onto Aunt Joy's street. Christmas lights shined from the rooftops of nearby houses like yummy-tummy gumdrops.

Warm air hit us when Aunt Joy's kids, Todd and Sandy—teenagers—opened the front door. Todd gave me a high five. Sandy put me in a headlock and rubbed her knuckles in my hair. Then she tickled me, spun me around, and did slow-motion karate moves—complete with grunts—that ended with a high five.

"Meghan!" Aunt Joy said, giving me a *squeeeeeezy* hug. "Last time I saw you, you were about two feet tall and missing a front tooth. You're growing up!"

"I can't help it," I said. "I tried growing down, but it didn't work."

"What a long day!" Mom said.

"I'm just glad you could stop to visit on your way to Texas and that you arrived here safely after that flat tire," Aunt Joy said. "I prayed for travel mercies. It looks like your guardian angels were with you."

"Angels watched us?" Kayla said. "Was it Gabriel and Duck?"

Aunt Joy looked puzzled.

"You really don't want to know," Mom

36

murmured. Then, chattering a mile a minute, they disappeared into the kitchen.

When Dad and Uncle Bob started hauling in the suitcases, I tugged on Sandy's arm. "I thought at least you would have snow. But it's December 23 and there's not a flake of snow anywhere! What's Christmas without snow?"

"The snow is a little late showing up this year," Sandy said. "They must be SLOW-flakes."

"Ha-ha," I said. "That was an ICE joke. Since there isn't any snow at all, they're NO-flakes. But if they come by Christmas, they'll be HO-HO-HO flakes."

Sandy nodded. "Not bad. There *is* snow in the weather forecast here, you know."

"What about Texas?" I asked.

Sandy shrugged. And my whole body

sagged like a wet napkin.

"Do you want to play foosball?" Sandy said.

"Yay!" Kayla cheered. "*Foosball* is a fun word!"

"It's a fun game too," I said, feeling less saggy.

Four foosball games, three sugary snacks, two hide-and-seek matches, and a cartoon in a pear tree later, I could barely keep my eyes open. I flopped on the couch while Kayla talked to her parents on Mom's cell phone. Then Mom sent Kayla and me to get ready for bed.

I wore my stripy, buzz-buzz pajamas. Kayla, of course, wore yellow duck pajamas with puffy duck slippers that actually quacked when she walked.

Mom and Dad planned on sleeping in the

guest bedroom. Kayla and I got the pull-out couch near the Christmas tree. I imagined how my secret surprise garland would look on Grandma's tree. It made me smile.

"I'll leave the tree lights on tonight," Aunt Joy said.

"They're like a huge night-light," I said.

"Exactly," Aunt Joy said. "Good night, girls."

Mom said prayers with Kayla and me. Then she kissed my forehead and gave Kayla a pat on the head.

Kayla held out Duck. "Duck wants a kiss too."

So Mom kissed Duck. "Anything else?" she asked.

"Duck misses his parents," Kayla said.

"I'm sure Duck's parents miss him too. Is Duck worried about them?"

Kayla made a face. "No, because then Duck would be chicken."

"I'm glad Duck isn't chicken," Mom said. "But will Duck have trouble sleeping?"

"Maybe," Kayla said in a small voice. "Can you sing Duck a song?"

Mom thought for a minute. "I used to sing one of my favorite Christmas songs to Meghan when she was a baby. It's a song about hope and waiting for the birth of a Savior. Do you remember it, Meghan?"

"Yes," I said. I didn't know what all the words meant. But it was a quiet, almost sad-sounding tune with whispery words. It always made me feel peaceful and safe.

In a low, slow voice, I started singing, "O come, O come, Emmanuel, and ransom captive Israel."

Mom sang, "That mourns in lonely exile

here, until the Son of God appear."

We both sang, "Rejoice! Rejoice! Emmanuel shall come to thee, O Israel."

Then, gently, gently, like a moonbeam's whisper, Mom hummed the melody over and over. I fell asleep to the glow of the Christmas lights, Kayla's soft breathing, and Mom's soft song drifting through the room like a kiss.

6

Let It Snow, Let It Snow ... Oh, Never Mind

"Wake up!" Kayla yelled, pouncing on me. She squished the *zzzzzs* right out of me.

"Get off!" I said, pushing her away.

"There's something you've got to see!" Kayla said.

I sat straight up. "SNOW?" I asked.

Kayla held Duck in my face. "No. This. Your Aunt Joy knit Duck a hat for Christmas!"

"Nice," I said, rubbing my eyes.

Aunt Joy poked her head into the room. "I didn't want Duck to be the only one without a present. We're opening *your* presents right after breakfast. Better hurry up!"

Let me tell you, I ate faster than a shooting star.

Then we opened fuzzy green Pickle-brand socks and pickle-scented lip gloss. We opened books, books, books! Plus, a whole lot more.

Finally Mom said, "Thanks for everything. It was so good to see you."

"Wait a minute!" I said. "That sounds like goodbye. We just got here. We're not leaving already, are we?"

"I'm afraid so," Aunt Joy said. "The weather is supposed to turn icy. You still have a ways to go, so I want you gone before the roads get bad."

"You mean . . . it's going to snow?" I asked.

Aunt Joy nodded.

"Whoopee!" I yelled. "Let it SNOW, let it SNOW, let it SNOW!"

While Dad packed the car *zip-zap-zoom-zippety-zoop,* snow started falling in thick, wet clumps.

Soon we hugged, waved goodbye, and pulled out of the driveway. Snow already covered the grass and sidewalks. The windshield wipers went WUMP-WUMP-WUMP, clearing off flecks of white as soon as they hit the glass.

As we drove, we listened to probably a million Christmas songs again. "Jingle Bells." "Winter Wonderland." "The Little

Drummer Boy." "What Child Is This?" "Away in a Manger." "Joy to the World." And of course . . . "Rudolph, the Red-Nosed Reindeer."

Finally we stopped for a bathroom break.

Icicles hung like monster teeth from the gas station. I blinked snow out of my eyes and stamped it off my shoes before I climbed back in the car.

When we pulled onto the highway again,

I nudged Kayla. "The windows steamed up. Let's draw on them."

With her pinkie finger, Kayla drew on the window. I wrote my name in big letters. Then I rubbed it off and looked out the window.

Snow was flying *everywhere,* falling fast like FLOW-flakes from a faucet. And not just snow, but something harder. Sleet?

My heart went BUMP-bump. It reminded me of a super-roller-coaster ride—scary and amazing at the same time. I made up a chant.

"Snow, snow, beautiful snow! Slippery and slick, fluffy and thick! Scoop it up, swoop it up, pat it like dough. Snow, snow, beautiful snow!"

I turned to Kayla. "Did you like my rhyme?"

Without looking at me, Kayla nodded.

I made a huffy sound. Because a no-look nod is not a five-star rating.

Mom glanced back at Kayla and frowned. Then she poked Dad on the shoulder. "Why don't you tell the girls the rest of the Christmas story?"

Kayla smiled. "Yes! Please, Mr. Thompson?"

"I don't know," Dad said. "It's getting really hard to see. And traffic is slowing down too."

"But . . . Duck would like it," Kayla said in a trembling voice.

"OK," Dad said. "If it will make Duck happy. Now, where did I stop?"

"At the stoplight," I said. "And good thing too, since it was red."

Dad laughed. "I meant in the story. Where did I leave off?"

"The angel that Kayla named Duck had just told Joseph to marry Mary," I said.

"Right," Dad said. "After that, the ruler of the land decided he needed a list of all the people he ruled."

"Why?" Kayla asked.

"He wanted to make sure everyone paid their taxes," Dad said. "So he ordered everyone to return to their hometowns and check in so he could count them. That meant Mary and Joseph had to travel to a city called Bethlehem. It was a very long trip, especially since they didn't have cars or planes back then. Mary rode on a donkey."

"Yuck," Kayla said. "I wouldn't want to travel by donkey. I'd want to travel by—"

"Duck," Dad finished for her. "Yes, we know."

Just then, I felt the car slide. Dad

WHOOP-DE-WHOOP straightened us out, but the car ahead of us slid into a ditch. So did the one in front of it.

"Call for help!" Dad said to Mom. He gripped the wheel and leaned forward. "Sorry, girls. The story has to wait. I need to focus on driving."

Mom made the phone call. Then she said, "Shouldn't we stop and help those cars in the ditch?"

"I'd love to," Dad said. "But I'm afraid if we stop, we'll get stuck too."

Suddenly, traveling by donkey or duck didn't seem so yucky anymore.

7

It Came, Came, Came upon a Midnight Clear

"So far I've counted seventeen cars off the road," I said an hour later.

Dad grunted. Leaning forward and gripping the wheel, he stared out the front window. Ever since it turned dark outside, it seemed he drove slower and slower. Plus, he had turned off the radio so he could concentrate on his driving. Now all we heard were the windshield wipers going WUMP-WUMP-WUMP and the crunch of our tires on the snow.

"How fast are we going?" I asked.

Mom frowned. "Maybe ten miles an hour."

"But we'll make it to Texas tonight, right?" I said.

The car slipped again. Mom gasped as Dad struggled with the wheel like a fisherman fighting a fish on his pole. He kept the car on the road.

"Duck's scared," Kayla whispered.

"Maybe we should stop," Mom said.

"But it's Christmas Eve!" I cried.

"And the roads are bad," Dad said in a tone hard as dirt. Then his voice softened. "Your mother is right. We'll exit here and find a hotel."

Mom looked unhappy when we pulled off. "The hotels are full."

"How do you know?" I asked.

"See that glowing sign?" Mom said, pointing. "It says *No Vacancy*. That means every room is taken. And they all say that."

"So . . . now what?" I said.

"We'll fill up at the gas station and use the bathroom," Dad said. "Then we'll keep driving. And we'll pray we can find a hotel we can stay in until the storm clears."

As Dad filled the gas tank, the worry lines on his forehead made my tummy do flip-flops. But Dad was a good driver. He'd keep us safe. Maybe the angels Gabriel and Duck would help too. I remembered what Aunt Joy had said, and I whispered a quick prayer. *Dear God, please keep us safe!*

Driving at a crawl, we passed four more exits. Each had hotels, but *No Vacancy* signs flashed at every one. So we kept going. And sliding. And counting cars off the road.

Soon, it was hard to see anything out the windows. Without the red taillights on the car in front of us showing the way, like Rudolph's nose, I felt sure the road itself would be lost.

"I bet Mary and Joseph didn't have to deal with icy roads," I said.

"True," Mom said. "But just like us, they had trouble finding a place to stay."

"Really?" Kayla said.

Mom nodded. "When they finally reached Bethlehem, so many people had come to have their names counted that all the places to stay overnight were full."

"They had hotels?" Kayla asked.

"The hotels were called inns," Mom said.

"But Mary was pregnant!" Kayla said. "Couldn't the hotel people let her rest on one of those soft couches in the lobby?"

Mom shook her head. "The inns in those days didn't have lobbies OR couches."

"Did they have indoor pools?" Kayla asked.

"No," Mom said. "But inns did have stables. That's where travelers kept their animals. And that's where Mary and Joseph finally stayed. After traveling so far, I'm sure they thought that simple stable was a blessing." She glanced out the window. "Right now, I'd be glad if *we* could find even a stable to sleep in tonight."

"Is a stable like a barn?" Kayla said.

"Back then, in that part of the world, a stable was more like a cave, with a dirt floor and hay," Mom said.

"Tell Kayla what happened next," I said.

Mom smiled. "Mary had her baby. Jesus,

the Son of God, was born in a stable! And his bed was the manger—the feeding trough—that held the animal's hay."

"I've never slept in an animal's food bowl," Kayla said. "But Mom said I sometimes slept in my car seat."

I felt the car slow down. Which was an amazing thing since we were already going slower than roadkill. Red and blue lights flashed in the dark night sky. "Police have the road blocked ahead," Dad said.

A pink-cheeked police officer, all bundled up like a package, waved us forward with a flashlight and signaled for Dad to put down his window. Icy air gusted into the car.

"We've had to close the interstate," the officer said.

"But we can't find a place to stay," Dad said.

The officer nodded. "There's a church off this exit that's taking in stranded travelers. Go right at the stop sign and follow the road about a quarter of a mile. You'll see the Open Door Church."

"But we *can't* stop," I cried, "or we'll *never* get to Texas on time! And the most important thing about Christmas besides presents and snow and family is ME putting up my special Meghan-made Christmas garland in Texas!"

"Sorry, kid," the officer said.

8

Deck the Fellowship Hall

Dad parked in a lot crowded with cars and snow. Carrying only what we needed, we walked carefully toward the entrance of the church. The air stung my face and crept down my shirt. Shivering, I looked down. I could tell the sidewalk had been shoveled and salted, but snow had swallowed it up again.

"We can't stay here," I complained. "What about my garland? Grandma and I were going to decorate on Christmas Eve."

"You'll have to wait," Mom said.

Which was not exactly the answer I wanted to hear.

"Come on in!" a woman called from doorway of the church. Her breath made puffs like smoke when she talked. She waved us forward. A black-and-white collie was next to her, jumping and barking and wagging his tail as if to say hello.

"Welcome, neighbors. I'm Debbie!" The woman's face wrinkled in a friendly smile. "I'm glad you made it safely here."

"We're grateful to have a place to stay," Mom said. "Thank you."

"But we're not your neighbors!" I blurted. And then my mouth kept right on going. "And you're not my Grandma Thompson. And it's not OK to be stuck in a church in the middle of nowhere with complete strangers on Christmas Eve!"

"Meghan Rose!" my mom said, with a wide-eyed look. "I'm very sorry, Debbie."

Debbie smiled at Mom and crouched down by me. "Sweetheart, you and I, we share the world, don't we? So that makes you my neighbor, doesn't it?"

I thought about that for a moment, then I nodded.

"And Jesus told us we should love our neighbors, right?"

I nodded again.

"And if you are my neighbor that I love, you can be my friend too, right?"

Once more I nodded.

Debbie clapped her hands. Her mittens made a dull THUMP-THUMP sound. "Good!" she said. "Then tonight you get to spend Christmas Eve with your family and neighbors and friends. And that's not so bad, is it?"

With a smile, I shook my head.

"Things will work out," Debbie added. "Now, do you see the man over there by the fellowship hall? That's Alton. He'll help you find a spot to sleep for tonight."

Feeling better, I grabbed Kayla's hand. Together, we led the way down the hall.

Alton stood by a table stacked with water bottles, snacks, and blankets. In the room behind him, I could see groups of people. Stranded families, just like ours. With blankets and suitcases spread all around, the room looked like a huge slumber party.

And it sounded like a crowd cheering at a football game. A baby cried. People talked on cell phones. Handheld electronics made rocket noises. Little kids ran around, most

of them screaming. All that noise bounced around the room so much that it seemed to hit me from everywhere all at once.

"How are we supposed to sleep with all this noise?" I asked.

Before anyone could answer, a booming voice blasted us. "I'm Alton," a man said. He shook Dad's hand and smiled at the rest of us. "Welcome."

"Thank you," Dad said. "You are an answer to prayer."

"Probably an answer to many prayers," Mom said. "There are lots of people here."

Alton chuckled. "There will always be room for one more at *this* inn. But you are quite right—we'll have a full house tonight. The good news is we don't expect to get many more. Fewer cars are on the interstate now, and other churches besides ours have opened their doors for stranded travelers."

"The bad news is I CAN'T HEAR MYSELF BREATHING," I said.

"How is it your church has all this water and all these blankets available?" Mom asked.

"Donations," Alton said. "Our pastor is a man of vision and action, and when he saw the weather forecast, he did the math. Lots of holiday travelers plus big snow and ice. He figured there were bound to be people who would need our help. So yesterday he contacted churches nearby, enlisted volunteers, and got things rolling. A local store gave a generous amount of supplies, and so did several church members. Now here we are, ready for the storm and right where I believe God wants us to be."

"Wowie," Kayla said. "Do you work

with the angels Gabriel and Duck?"

That comment, believe it or not, made Alton burst with a hearty laugh that sounded an awful lot like HO-HO-HO. "I work with anyone willing to help others, no matter who they are," he finally choked out. "It's my way of showing God's love."

Kayla smiled. "I think the angels would like you, Mr. Giant Laughing Man."

9

Not-So-Silent Night

Alton showed us where the restrooms were. After that, Mom collected blankets, Dad took four water bottles, and Kayla and I picked out snacks. We found an empty spot in the hall to set our things. The floor was hard, but at least it was warm and dry.

Still, all the people, all the movement, all the NOISE worried me. It didn't feel like a safe, cozy Christmas Eve. Instead it felt crazy and confusing. It didn't smell like peppermint and sugar cookies. Instead it smelled like dinner leftovers, and my stomach growled. My special garland was nowhere in sight. Instead there were suitcases piled everywhere.

Maybe this is how Mary felt when she had to stay in the stable full of animals, I thought. That idea made me feel a little better.

Before the lights in the fellowship hall went out for the evening, Alton, Debbie, and several other workers came in. Using a portable microphone Alton gave the whole group instructions for the morning. Then Alton introduced Pastor Paul, who told us he wanted to share a Christmas story in the sanctuary. Any who cared to listen were welcome. "Though we are not at home, the spirit of Christmas still dwells here," he said.

His words worked like magic. Nearly

everyone filed into the rows of pews.

Pastor Paul opened his Bible and began to read. His story started just like Dad had said, with a visit from an angel to Mary.

Pastor Paul read about Mary and Elizabeth, about Joseph and his dream, and about traveling to Bethlehem. I nudged Kayla when he got to the part she hadn't heard yet, the part that comes after Jesus was born. I wanted to make sure she didn't miss it.

"That night in the fields near Bethlehem some shepherds were guarding their sheep. All at once an angel came down to them from the Lord, and the brightness of the Lord's glory flashed around them. The shepherds were frightened. But the angel said, 'Don't be afraid! I have good news for you, which will make everyone happy. This very day in

King David's hometown a Savior was born for you. He is Christ the Lord. You will know who he is, because you will find him dressed in baby clothes and lying on a bed of hay.'

"Suddenly many other angels came down from heaven and joined in praising God. . . .

"After the angels had left and gone back to heaven, the shepherds said to each other, 'Let's go to Bethlehem and see what the Lord has told us about.' They hurried off and found Mary and Joseph, and they saw the baby lying on a bed of hay.

"When the shepherds saw Jesus, they told his parents what the angel had said about him. Everyone listened and was surprised. But Mary kept thinking about all this and wondering what it meant" (Luke 2:8-13, 15-19).

Pastor Paul closed his Bible. "This special time gives us many things to treasure in our hearts, like Mary did. Perhaps the most important thought is that Jesus was born in an unexpected situation in an unexpected place to unexpected people. He was born a man, yet he was *God*. Through his life, he built a bridge between God and people and made sure we could someday cross that bridge too, if we want to. This Christmas, we celebrate the birth of a Savior and a king."

"Wow," Kayla whispered to me. "Now THAT'S a great Christmas story."

"And it doesn't have an expiration date," I whispered back.

Debbie started singing "Silent Night." One by one, people joined in.

This was a different kind of noise than I

had heard recently. Thankful noise. Heartfelt noise. Noise that felt right for the first time all day.

And that made me curious about what Mary thought about in her heart the night the shepherds visited.

I bet Mary wasn't thinking about snow. Or the fact that she was staying in a noisy, crowded stable far from family. Or whether or not she would get to decorate a tree with a garland.

I bet all Mary thought about was Jesus. And then BLAM! It hit me. Mary got it right! The most important thing about Christmas wasn't presents or snow or decorations. It was Jesus. Only Jesus. He was all that ever really mattered in the first place.

I said a quick prayer. *Dear God. I'm sorry I forgot the most important thing about*

Christmas. Thank you for Jesus. Thank you, thank you, thank you.

I imagined my prayer floating up with the song to the ceiling, dancing down through the hallway, and softly slipping out into the night.

Long after we left the sanctuary and my parents and Kayla and I were snuggled together under our borrowed blankets, the noise from people around me kept me awake. A baby still cried. I heard snoring. Someone's phone rang. The collie barked whenever someone got up to go to the bathroom. More than ever, I felt like a stranger in a strange land.

But that was OK because just like Mary and Joseph sleeping in the stable, I had Jesus. And on that not-so-silent night, he was enough to make everything else OK.

I Heard the Bing-bong Bells

Bing-bong-bong-bong-bing-bong . . .

Church bells. I could almost feel them ringing "Joy to the World." What a cool way to wake up on Christmas morning!

Something soft landed THUNK on my head. *Someone* giggled.

I opened one eye. "Kayla, did you put Duck on my face?"

"Duck wanted to wake you up, so he attacked your nose," Kayla said.

I sat up. "Duck woke me up at the *quack*

of dawn. AND I smell something yummy."

"The church is serving pancakes at the other end of the fellowship hall," Mom said.

"Duck likes pancakes," Kayla said.

The line moved quickly. Still, it wasn't the same as breakfast with my family. "Texas seemed a long way off before we started our trip," I said. "But it seems even further away today."

"Duck feels the same way about my parents," Kayla said. "But I told Duck to relax. They're calling me again tonight. I hope we're in Texas by then."

My heart went BUMP-bump. "Dad, are the roads open now?"

"I drove in this morning in my pickup," a server said as she handed me a plate of steaming pancakes. "Even though the interstate is still closed here, the back roads are open. You could take them until you find a place to get back on the interstate."

"Why are the back roads clear but not the interstate?" Mom asked

"Most local people plowed their own driveways and then simply kept on going," the server said. "You can take those back roads for about thirty miles and then get back on the interstate. It's probably clear further south."

"It's worth a try," Dad said. "With any luck, we'll get to Texas by early evening."

"Yay!" I said. "Then I can finally decorate!"

"Will you spend Christmas Day with your family?" Mom asked the server.

"We'll celebrate after we get everyone here safely on the road again," she said.

"Won't everyone leave today?" I asked.

The server shook her head. "Some people don't have the proper tires to travel when the roads are still slick. They won't take a chance. They'll stick around one more day."

Frowning, I glanced around the fellowship hall. How many kids would stay behind? Maybe they'd feel better about Christmas if the hall felt a little bit more like home.

Then BLAM! I had an idea. I tugged Mom's arm and whispered in her ear.

Mom smiled. "Let's ask Alton if that's OK. I'll send Dad outside to get it."

"Get what?" Kayla asked.

"You'll see," I said. "Let's find Alton."

Alton was in the kitchen washing dishes.

"Alton," I said. "I want to help."

Alton held up soapy hands. "That's sweet, but I've got it covered."

"No, not like that!" I said, shaking my head. "I want make the fellowship hall look more like a family Christmas."

"And how are you going to do that?" he said.

I took a big breath. Was I really willing to give up my special surprise for a group of strangers?

But didn't God do that for us? Give up his Son to a group of strangers? Giving up my garland would be my gift back to God.

"I made a special paper-chain garland," I said. "It's as long as a jump rope. If you have some paper, you can cut more paper strips, and everyone left behind can make their own chains and add it to mine. The chain will grow and grow and grow. Then you can hang it across the room. It'll make the room feel more like home."

Alton broke into a giant-sized where-did-your-lips-go? smile. "I love your idea," he said. "We can cut up old church bulletins and loop them together. It will be a wonderful reminder of God's love, which connects us all!"

Just then, Dad came into the kitchen, carrying my garland.

We ended up sticking around the church an extra hour. It was fun helping kids hook loops together and watching the chain grow. It was hard, *hard*, HARD to give up my garland, but Grandma and Grandpa Thompson could help me make a new one when we got to their house.

We made it to Texas before dark. Texas didn't have any snow, but I didn't care. Kayla's parents called to talk to Kayla, and we found out Kayla's grandma was feeling much better! We ate a Texas-sized dinner, which tasted almost as good as our pancake breakfast. We opened presents, which made a mess. And then we used the wrapping-paper mess to make a WHOO-HOO! brand-new garland!

Just like Mary, Jesus' mother, in my heart I thought about all the things I had learned about Jesus this Christmas. I strung my thoughts together like a paper chain. Best of all, I knew I could add to the chain day after day. All year long, to be exact.

After all, the Christmas story doesn't have an expiration date.

Chatter Matters

1. Read the Christmas story found in Luke 1 and 2. Which parts of the story sound familiar? What is your favorite part? Why?

2. A tradition is something that is passed down or done year after year. What Christmas traditions does your family have? Which one is your favorite?

3. Kayla was apart from her mom and dad. Have you ever had to spend time apart from a loved one because he or she was traveling or working or deployed? How did you feel? If not, how could you encourage a friend who has to spend time apart from a loved one?

4. Meghan and Kayla sang a lot of Christmas songs. List some of your favorite Christmas melodies. What stories do they tell about Christmas? Do you think any of them would make a nice lullaby like "O Come, O Come, Emmanuel"?

5. Meghan says the Christmas story never expires. What ways could you celebrate the Christmas story all year long?

Blam! – Great Activity Ideas

1. Get a group of friends together and go caroling. Consider visiting a retirement home to help spread joy to the elderly.

2. Make your own paper-chain Christmas garland. Cut six-by-one-inch strips of regular construction paper or, for a fancier garland, cut strips of shiny, two-sided wrapping or scrapbook paper. Put glue on the tip of a strip, curl the strip into a loop, and hold the ends together until they stick. Slip another strip of paper through the loop you just made. Glue, curl, and hold. Repeat until your garland reaches the length you want.

3. Make your own Christmas stamps. Hot-glue small foam winter shapes onto the flat end of a plastic bottle cap. Once dry, press the shape into an ink pad (or color it with a marker), then stamp the image on cards, paper towels, or gift tags. You can even stamp on a sheet of white paper to create your own wrapping paper.

4. The Open Door Church was prepared to help during a crisis. Find out ways you and your friends can donate food, blankets, clothing, or other supplies to organizations that assist people in need during the holiday season.

5. Meghan made up a chant about snow. Make up your own poem about snow.

For my Stilly friends—LZS
For Michaela, Jacob, and Mallory—SC

Lori Z. Scott graduated from Wheaton College eons ago. She is a teacher, a wife, the mother of two busy teenagers, and a writer. In her spare time, Lori loves doodling and making up lame jokes. You can find out more about her books at www.MeghanRoseSeries.com.

Stacy Curtis is a cartoonist, illustrator, printmaker, and twin who's illustrated over twenty children's books, including a *New York Times* best seller. He and his wife, Jann, live in the Chicago area and happily share their home with their dogs, Derby and Inky.